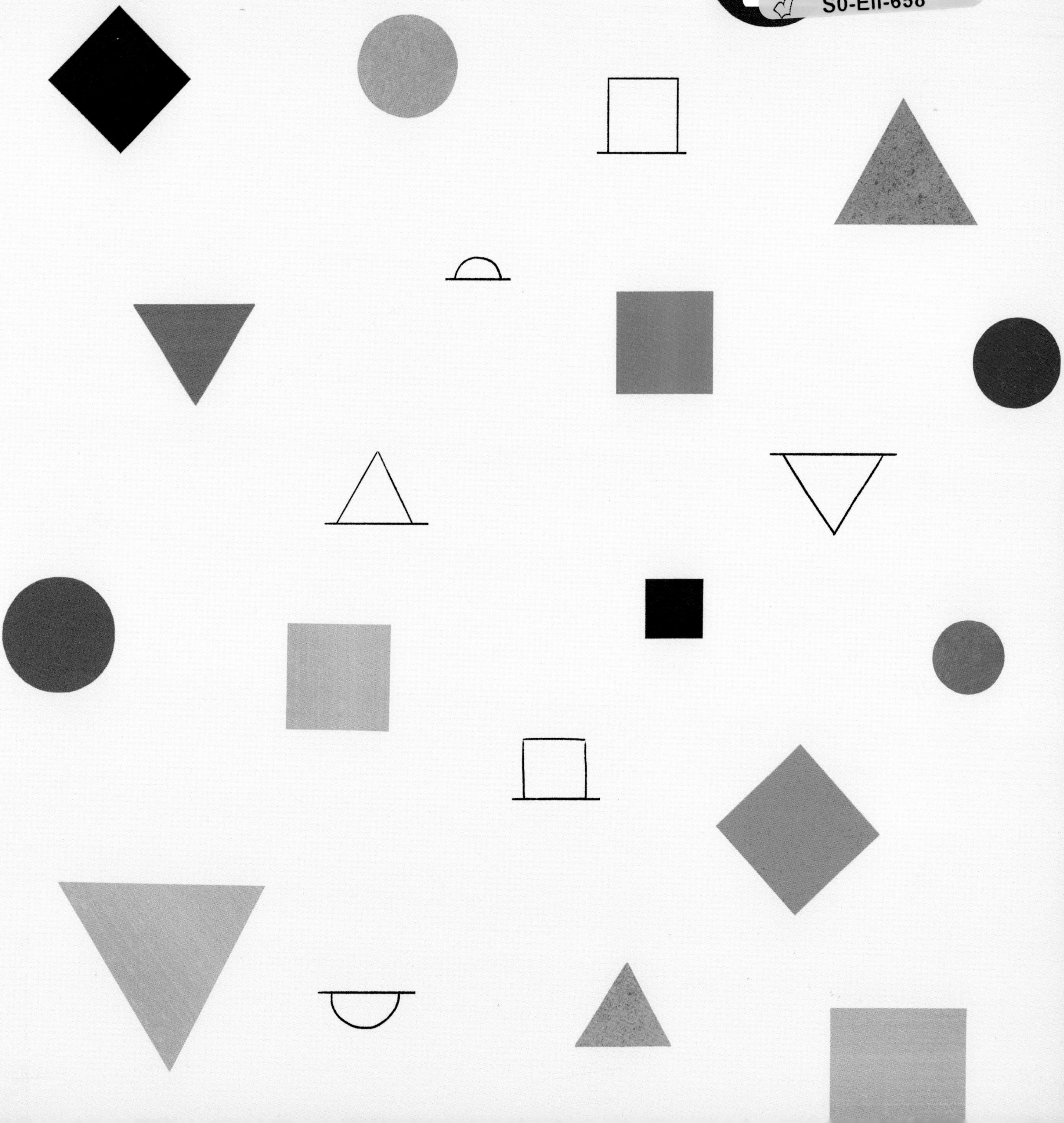

Originally published as *De wereld van Worm. Vormen* in Belgium and the Netherlands by Clavis Uitgeverij, 2021
English translation from the Dutch by Clavis Publishing Inc., New York

Copyright © 2022 Clavis Publishing Inc., New York

Visit us on the Web at www.clavis-publishing.com.

The World of Worm. Shapes written and illustrated by Esther van den Berg

ISBN 978-1-60537-793-3

This book was printed in April 2022 at Nikara,
M. R. Štefánika 858/25, 963 01 Krupina, Slovakia.

First Edition
10 9 8 7 6 5 4 3 2 1

Clavis Publishing supports the First Amendment and celebrates the right to read.

Esther van den Berg

The World of Worm
Shapes

Clavis

NEW YORK

Worm is awake and starts his day.

Time for morning gymnastics.
That's how **Worm** stays in good shape.

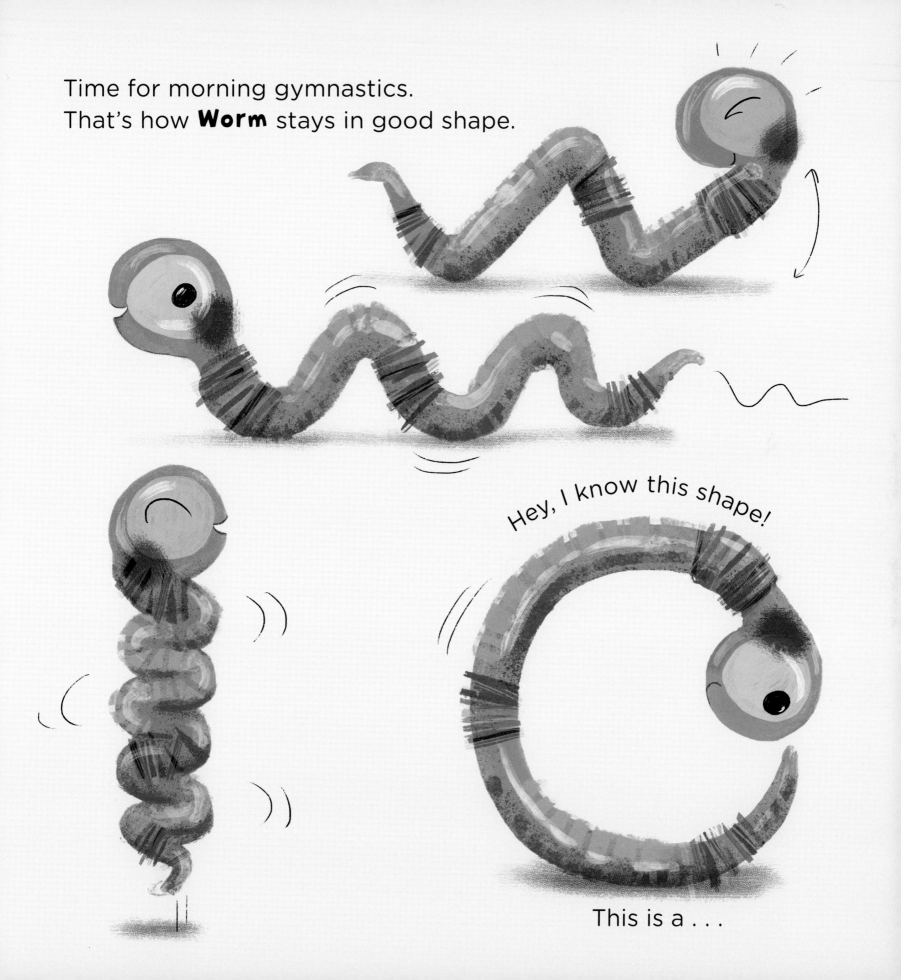

Hey, I know this shape!

This is a . . .

. . . circle!

There are more **circles** on the right.

Which do you like best?
But watch out . . . there's one you can't eat!

Is your tummy full, **Worm?**
Let's go outside then!

Look, even more **circles.**

Hey, this isn't a **circle!**
This is a . . .

. . . square!

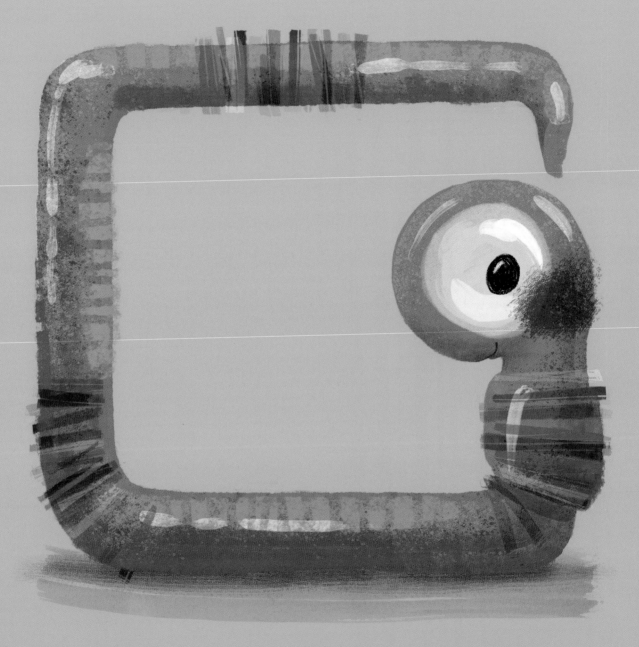

There are more **squares** on the right.

All of these **squares** are for playing.
Which do you like best?

Are you done playing, **Worm?**
Let's move on then!

Look, even more **squares.**

. . . triangle!

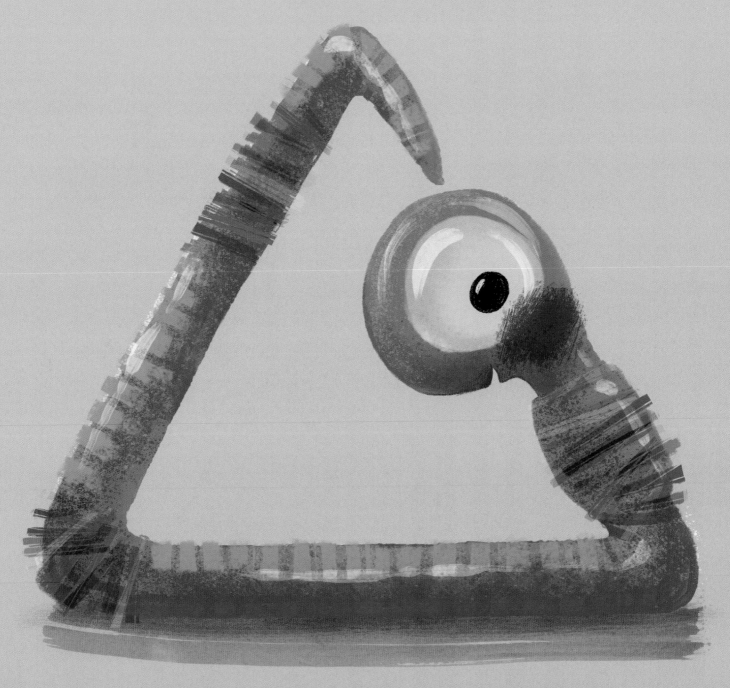

There are more **triangles** on the right.

All of these **triangles** make sounds.
Which ones are loud? And which ones are quiet?
(And what sound does a worm make?)

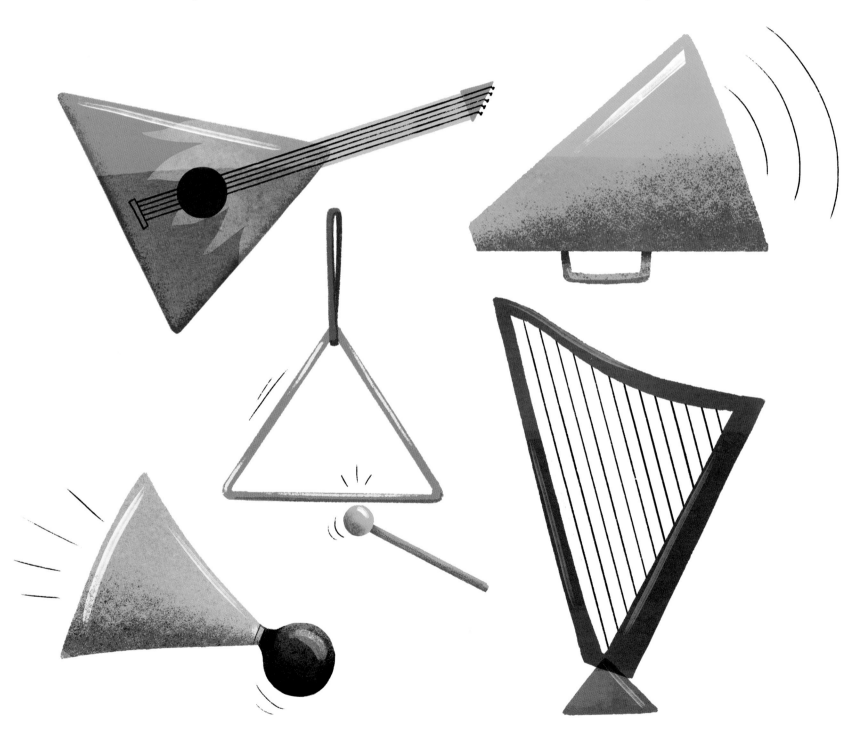

Look, even more **triangles.**

Hey, this isn't a **triangle!**
This is a . . .

...heart!

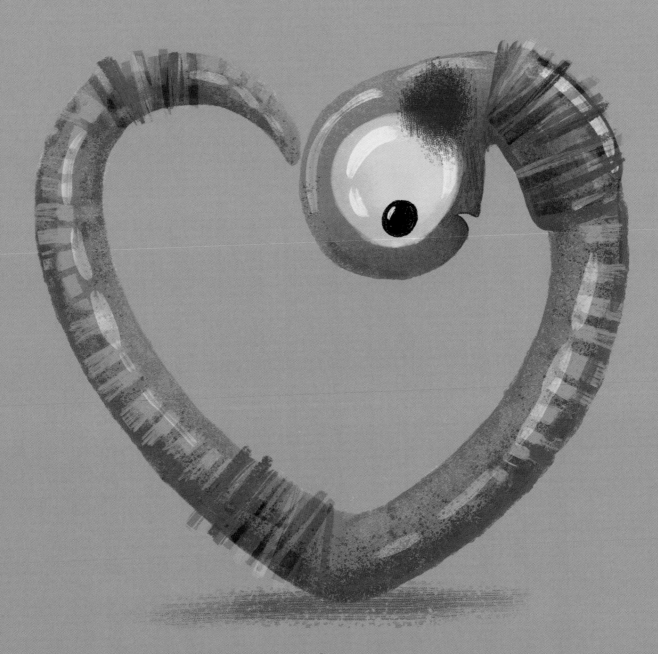

There are more **hearts** on the right.

All of these **hearts** are found in nature.
Which do you like best?

Look, even more **hearts.**

Hey, this isn't a **heart!**

This is a . . .

...star!

It was a beautiful day.
Are you tired too, **Worm?**

Worm is getting ready to go to sleep.

Will you turn off the light?

Look, even more **stars.**

Good night, **Worm.**